THE CURSED LIBRARY

ABHYA SONI

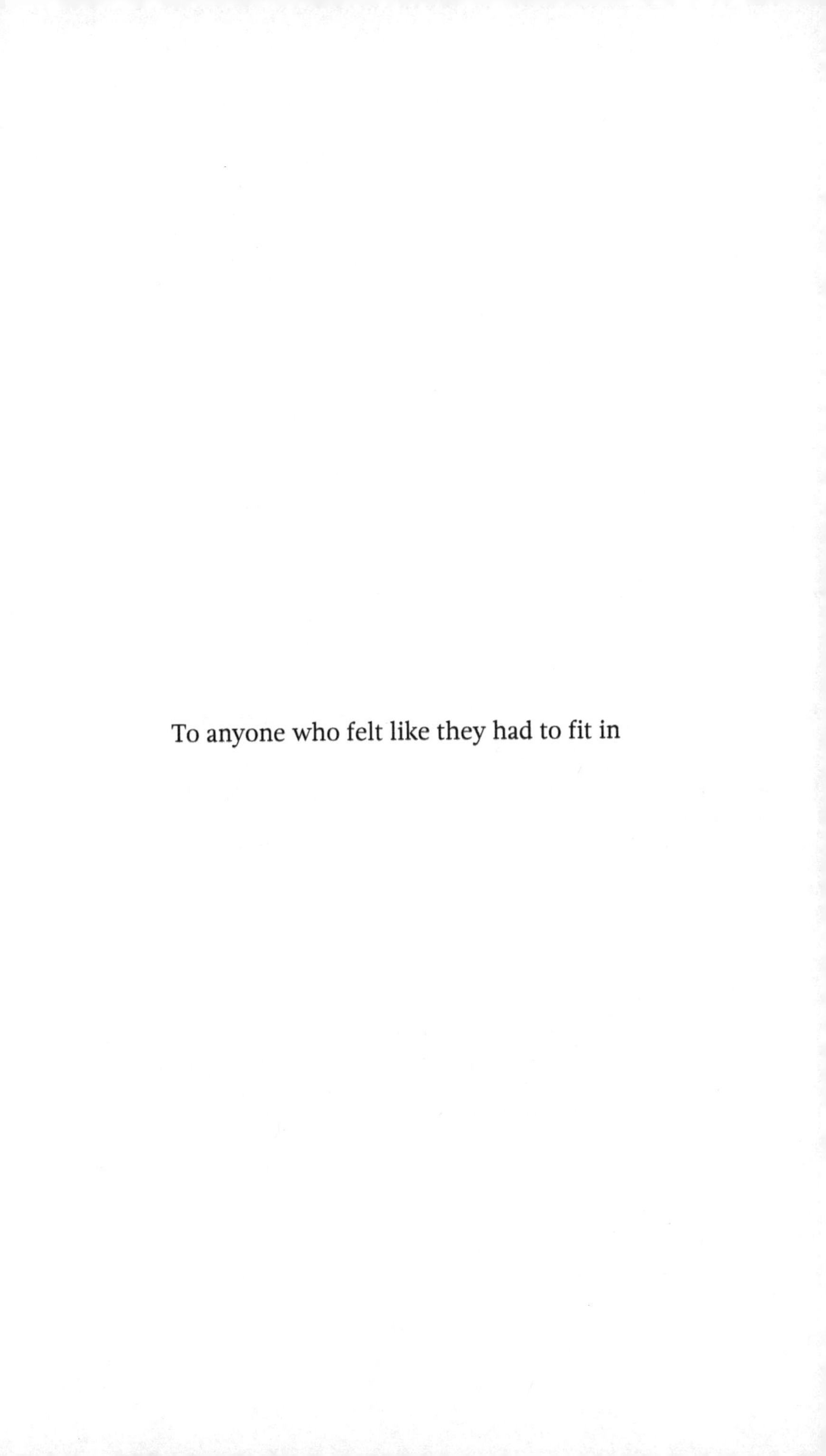

To anyone who felt like they had to fit in

Contents

Disclaimer

The author affirms that this is a light-hearted book intended for entertainment purposes only. All characters, locations, incidents, events, are purely fictitous in nature and any resemblance bearing to the above is a mere coincidence and have no connection whatsoever to reality. The book does not intend to hurt, discredit or demean the feelings of any person, community or any section of society.

CHAPTER I

The story starts here

In the quiet corner of the school library, Hope sat with her head bowed, her fingers tracing the edges of her notebook. The sting of the latest encounter with her arch nemesis, Amber, still fresh in her mind. Hope's eyes welled up with tears as she replayed the cruel words and mocking laughter. Each insult felt like a dagger, piercing her heart and leaving her feeling small and insignificant. Her stomach churned at the thought of facing Amber again. The fear of another confrontation made her dread the next school day, casting a shadow over her once safe haven. A spark of anger flickered within her. Why did Amber always target her? The frustration of being unable to stop the bullying gnawed at her, making her clench her fists in helpless rage. Hope glanced around the library, seeing groups of friends chatting and laughing. She felt a pang of loneliness, wishing she had someone to confide in, someone who understood her pain. She wiped away a tear, feeling a wave of embarrassment. The thought of others witnessing her humiliation made her cheeks burn with shame. She wondered if they saw her as weak or deserving of the bullying. Hope's mind swirled with confusion. What had she done to deserve this? Self-doubt crept in, making her question her worth and whether she was somehow to blame for Amber's cruelty. As she sat there, lost in her thoughts, a gentle hand rested on her shoulder. It was her friend, Asher, who had noticed Hope's distress. "Hey, are you okay?" Asher asked softly, his eyes full of concern. "No." She replied, quietly. The echoes of the bullies' cruel laughter still lingered in the air. Asher's heart ached seeing his friend in such pain. He knelt beside her, gently placing a hand on her shoulder. Hope looked up, her eyes red and puffy. "Why do they hate me so much?" she whispered, her voice breaking. Asher shook his head, his expression firm. "They don't hate you. They're just... mean. And wrong. You don't deserve any of this." He reached into his backpack and pulled out a small, crumpled tissue, offering it to her. Hope took it with a shaky hand, wiping her tears. Asher sat down next to her, their backs against the wall. "Look, I know Amber isn't the kindest person we know, but I'm your friend. I'll always have your back." Asher smiled. "Thanks, Asher." "Anytime, Hope."

CHAPTER II

An article

Colston Library Closed!

Authorities have closed Colston library permanently due to complaints of eerie noises, paranormal activities, and laughter of children at night after closing time.

Officer Runt has given a testimony regarding the same. "My fellow officers and I have examined the whole library. We have not found anything to prove that there are paranormal activities inside the building but we have found out that books are falling out of fixed positions and there are some unexplainable noises and activities which have been noticed in the left wing of the library. At 3PM, Tuesday afternoon, we came across five books which had fallen over a table while we were investigating. I had laid them down on the table, the front cover facing the ceiling. Ten minutes later, those same books fell onto the ground. Nobody was near the table nor the books." The police has everyone hooked to know what the Colston library holds. "In the left wing, my colleagues were investigating, when they heard a small child crying. Judging by the pitch of the voice, it seemed to be a child no older than 5 years. They went to see if anyone was there. When they finally got to the place where the crying was coming from, nobody was there."

"No phones at dinner, Hope!" Mrs. Eldrod set down white plates on the dining table. "Sorry, mom. I was reading the latest article. It's about the Colston library." Hope kept her phone down on the table, "did you know that it's been permanently closed?"

"Too bad. I have lots of memories in that library. I used to go there all the time with my friends in college. I read a lot of helpful books there." Mr. Eldrod said, his eyebrows furrowed.

"Yeah. Why are they closing it anyway?" Mrs. Eldrod sat down. "The article said that because of some complaints about eerie noises, books falling down, paranormal activity and laughter of children, they're closing."

"What nonsense! It's probably some reckless middle schoolers playing pranks. It's a shame that the adults here believe any rubbish." Mr. Eldrod exclaimed.

"I wouldn't be so sure that it's just a bunch of middle schoolers. Eerie noises, laughter of children and books falling down are still believable, but paranormal activities?" Mrs. Eldrod squinted her eyes. "Well, the laughter of children came from the library after closing hours. I bet it's probably some high schoolers playing pranks. It's too bad the place is closing. I had a whole list of books I wanted to read over the summer!" Hope sighed. Her phone vibrated. It was a notification.

Colston library book sale!

After police investigation, officers have come to conclusion that regardless of whether they find anything or not, they will still close the library for the betterment of the society. "We will just say that the library has served all of us long enough. Although, it would be a shame if the books would be locked up, for no one to access. We have decided that on Sunday, we will give a chance to everyone to buy books of their choice." Officer Runt has stated.

Liam Colston has given a statement saying, "I'm very disappointed about what is happening to my poor library. I remember all the adults who live abroad now coming into my library as kids, in search of either the latest comic books or a ridiculously thick book for school. I am happy these books will be sold, but I am truly sorry for its closing."

Hope read the article and smiled. "What is it, Hope?" Mrs. Eldrod asked. "They're holding a book sale on Sunday to, hopefully, clear out all the books in the library!" Hope grinned. "How lovely!" "We should all go, then." Mr. Eldrod crossed his arms. "Yes! Hope, you should ask Asher if he's coming too." "I'm not sure he will, mom." Hope squinted her eyes. "Tell him to come if he isn't coming. Your mom and I can make lunch after we go. Bribe him with food." Mr.

Eldrod joked. Hope and Mrs. Eldrod laughed. "I'll ask him after dinner." Hope said.

CHAPTER III

Biscuits

On Sunday, Hope and her parents were at the book sale, along with the rest of the town. They were inside the library. The walls were brown, the tiles chipping off the floor. Hope had told Asher to come and he had agreed, so she knew to look for him. Her parents were checking out the books about finance while Hope stood there in her blue jeans, her green top, and her chestnut-brown hair reaching the end of her ears. She saw him. He was walking up to her, his black jeans swaying as he walked, his gray shirt full of wrinkles. He brushed his hand through his messy black hair. "Hey, Hoppy." "Hi. You didn't bring anyone with you, right?" Hope answered, looking around. "Just me and my folks." "Good." Asher had a habit of bringing his friends to places Hope had invited him. He didn't understand that Hope and his friends didn't exactly get along too well. They would pick on Hope in school because of her freckles. "Look, I know you don't like my friends. I'm not going to invite them anymore." "I really hope so. You don't know what they've done to me." "I know, I know." Asher looked down. "Anyway, mom and dad are making lunch in the backyard today, after the book sale. You wanna come?" Hope rolled her eyes. "Yes, please! Your dad's homemade burgers are the bomb!" Asher smiled. "Great!" Hope grinned. They both went to the college books. Hope wanted to study law and Asher wanted to be a geophysicist. "Ash! Look, two volumes about how to be pass the bar exam!" "You're kidding! Look! Two volumes of the fundamentals of geophysics!" Asher replied. Hope looked at him, her face saying 'what?' "Why are you looking at me like that?" Asher smiled, confused. "Nothing. I'm just wondering how someone can get excited about two whole books about physics." Hope answered. "Oh no." Asher's smile faded away. "What is it?" Hope asked. "Amber, five o'clock!" He warned. Amber was one of the girls who didn't like Hope. Hope wasn't too popular at their high school. She wasn't the most liked either. Amber was walking towards them, in her long pink dress, her long auburn-brown hair was let down in all its glory. "Would you look at that, it's Joke and Asher. I would've expected to see you in the children's section, Joke. You know, because you act like such a baby." "Hey, her name's *Hope*!" Asher defended. "Asher! You're really going to defend her?" Amber looked surprised. "I'll defend her for as long as I need to." Asher replied. "Wow. You know, being Josh and Evan's friend, I thought you would make better decisions about who you hang out with and who you stay away from." Amber rolled her eyes, twisting her hair with her finger. "I don't need my friends to tell me who to hang out with and who to stay away from. I'm good at deciding that myself." Asher folded his arms. "Oh, honestly, your sarcasm is awful." Amber scoffed. "Thank you. Come on, Hope." He grabbed Hope's arm and took her to the fictional section.

✳✳✳

After the book sale, Hope and her parents took Asher and his parents to their house. "It's been a while since we've had you guys over! Asher and Hope meet often, but we should meet too!" Mrs. Eldrod said. "I agree! We always have such a fun time with you guys!" Mrs. Hayes said. The parents went to the kitchen to get all the supplies to make burgers, while Hope and Asher sat down on the chairs they had in the backyard. "Which book are you going to read first?" Asher asked. "I think I'll read the storybooks first. I'm not sure about the law books just yet. I want to read them before college, so I can be less tired." Hope chuckled. "That's a good strategy, I guess. What are you going to do about Amber?" "I don't know. She's too much work for me to fix." "Well, whatever you're gonna do, I'll help you. "Alright, kids! Get ready for some Eldrod-Hayes special burgers and brownies!" Mr. Eldrod cheered. "Alright, we'll get started on the brownie batter, while you both grill the patty for the burger." Mrs. Hayes said. "Yes!" Mrs. Eldrod agreed. "Dad, where'd you keep the poker cards?" Hope got up. "I think they're in the game cupboard. If they're not there, try my study." Mr. Eldrod said, getting the burger buns out of the packaging. "Alright. Ash, you wanna come?" "Sure." Asher and Hope went upstairs, down the hall to the left. There was a room in their house which nobody had used. Hope's parents decided to put all of their extra things in the room. One of their cupboards was full of board games that Hope's parents had 'collected' over the years. "I still can't believe this cupboard's still so organized." Asher laughed. "I know. Mom really doesn't skip out on keeping this place clean. There isn't a speck of dust on anything." Hope agreed, scanning the cupboard, in search of the poker cards. Asher went over to the window sill. "Look at that brat. Sitting on her chair, as if she has everything she could ever ask for." Asher said, looking at Amber as she sat on her swing-hammock-chair. She was listening to something using her headphones and was simultaneously reading a book. "Ash, considering the amount of money both her parents have, I'm pretty sure she does have everything she could ask for." Hope said, the cards in her hands. "Unfortunately, that's true." Asher shook his head. "Now, let's leave the monstrosity alone. We have burgers to eat."

Hope smiled. She took Asher downstairs, into the backyard. "Got, it?" Mr. Eldrod asked. "Yep," Hope waved the cards in the air. "Great. You guys get started. Once we're done, start a new game for us." Mr. Hayes said. "The brownies are browning. How're the burgers?" Mrs. Eldrod came from the kitchen with Mrs. Hayes. "The patties are done; the buns are done and so are the veggies. We're just using the leftover onions to clean the grill." Mr. Eldrod said.

After lunch, everyone sat down to play poker. "Full house." Mr. Hayes slyly smiled. Everyone groaned. "Hope, your turn." "Royal flush." Hope laid out her cards on the table. "Yes!" Asher exclaimed. "How do you feel, Paul?" Mrs. Hayes chuckled. "That's my girl!" Mr. Eldrod cheered. "Hope Jane Eldrod. You have won today's poker match!" Mrs. Eldrod smiled. Everyone clapped. "Good game. Nice poker face, Hope. I really thought I won for a second!" Mr. Hayes laughed. "I was trying really hard not to laugh!" Hope agreed. Asher and his parents got up, ready to leave. "Hey, can we meet in the park tomorrow?" "Sure, why?" Hope said. Asher looked at their parents, to make sure they weren't paying attention, "my dad wants me to go to fishing with him. Either that, or he tutors me. I don't want to do either of those things, so, I'm trying to make as many plans as possible." He whispered. "That sounds like something you would do. Don't worry. I'll come." Hope rolled her eyes. "Thank you so much! You're a life saver!" Asher smiled. "Asher, come on!" Mrs. Hayes called. "Bye, Hoppy." Asher grinned. "Bye, Ash." Hope waved. Once they left, Hope went up to her room. She let out a sigh as she saw her wine-colored wall, her white cupboards and her bed, calling her name. *One nap couldn't hurt anyone, right?* She plopped herself onto her bed, switched on her air conditioner and fell asleep.

***

After a long two hours, Hope woke up. Her hair was a mess and her eyes were barely open. She got up, brushed her hair and washed her face. She was going downstairs when she heard her mother talking to someone at the door. "Why, thank you! I can't believe you took out the time to make us these biscuits!" She was saying. Hope slowly went down the stairs, hoping to not be heard or seen. "It's not a problem! I love baking, you see." Another woman said. Hope's eyes widened. It was Amber's mother. She gave Mrs. Eldrod a tin full of biscuits. "You know, since Amber and Hope are such good friends, I thought you guys wouldn't mind if I stopped by and gave you these." She smiled. *No we're not! Amber and I barely get along! Why would she say that to mom?! Look at her, smiling like she's plotting our murder in her mind. Wait, what if she put poison in those biscuits?! She's capable of doing it!* Her mind raced, suspicions clouding her thoughts like storm clouds gathering on the horizon. Was this some sort of trap, a guise to gain access to her home under the pretense of goodwill? Or perhaps it was a genuine peace offering, an attempt to break the chaos between their families. "Oh, well, Hope and I will devour these biscuits before sunrise tomorrow morning!" Mrs. Eldrod laughed. "I sure hope so!" Amber's mom said, "well, I better get going. Enjoy the biscuits!" She waved and left. Hope went to her mother. "Mom! Why did you take those biscuits!?"

"What do you mean? Amber's mother came and gave these to us!"

"No! Don't eat those!" Hope snatched the tin from her. She opened it and sniffed them.

"Whatever are you doing?"

"They don't smell like poison..."

"Poison!? Why would you think that?!" Mrs. Eldrod took the tin back from Hope.

"Mom, me and Amber do not get along! She always bullies me!"

"What nonsense! Her mother tells you both are wonderful friends! Why else would she bring us biscuits?"

"To poison us, mom!"

"That's ridiculous! What does Amber say to you, anyway?"

"She calls me 'Joke' instead of 'Hope', says I act like a baby, and she says my freckles look like a connect-the-dots puzzle."

Mrs. Eldrod was stunned. "My, my, my. She's that rude to you?"

"Yes! That's why I'm telling you, mom, don't eat those biscuits!"

"Well, I don't know what do with them!"

"Just throw them away, mom!"

"Are you sure?"

"Yes!"

Mrs. Eldrod went to their trash can and threw away the biscuits. Hope watched her as she dumped them in. *Thank god that's over with. I should tell Asher about this.* "I'm going upstairs." "Alright, sweetie. Listen, if Amber does anything else to you, tell me, okay? I will give her and her mother a piece of my mind!" Mrs. Eldrod said. "Mom, please don't do that." Hope said, walking up the stairs. She went into her room and snatched her phone from her bed. She dialed Asher's number. When Hope called, Asher was sound asleep. His phone's ringtone jolted him up. "Asher Hayes." He very slightly managed to mumble out of himself. "Ash! You will never believe who was just at my door!" Hope started. "Who?" Asher yawned. "Have you just woken up?" "Kinda," "Oh. Well, Amber's mom was just at my door and she handed mom a tin of biscuits!" "And?" "And? What do you mean, and?" Hope sounded confused. "Hoppy, if she gave you biscuits, she gave you biscuits. Just eat them and move on." Asher rubbed his eye. "Ash! You out of all people should understand that if you get offerings from the enemy, there can never be peace on the battlefield." Hope said. Asher didn't say a word and hung up. "Hello? Ash? Asher?" She threw her phone on her bed and sat on the ground, her hands aggressively tangling her hair.

CHAPTER IV

Hope's a friend

As he stepped through the front door, the weight of exhaustion settled heavily upon Asher's shoulders. The afternoon sun had sapped his energy, leaving him feeling drained after spending hours at Hope's house. His once cheerful attitude had wilted like a flower in the heat, replaced by a languid slouch as he trudged towards his room. With a weary sigh, Asher collapsed onto his bed, the soft mattress offering little relief from the exhaustion that engulfed him. His eyelids drooped heavily, threatening to surrender to the want of sleep despite the midday hour. The scent of the Eldrod's cooking lingered in the air, a bittersweet reminder of the laughter shared over lunch. He dozed off, care-free about anything else which was happening.

***

When Hope called, Asher was sound asleep. His phone's ringtone jolted him up. "Asher Hayes." He very slightly managed to mumble out of himself.

"Ash! You will never believe who was just at my door!" Hope started.

"Who?" Asher yawned.

"Have you just woken up?"

"Kinda,"

"Oh. Well, Amber's mom was just at my door and she handed mom a tin of cookies!"

"And?"

"And? What do you mean, and?" Hope sounded confused.

"Hoppy, if she gave you cookies, she gave you cookies. Just eat them and move on." Asher rubbed his eye. "Ash! You out of all people should understand that if you get offerings from the enemy, there can never be peace on the battlefield." Hope said. "Asher Elijah Hayes!" Mrs. Hayes yelled. Asher's eyes widened. He immediately hung up and rolled out of his bed. He ran downstairs only to see his mom sitting on the sofa, watching television. "Mom?" Asher whispered. "Asher! It's almost 6PM! You've been sleeping forever! How will you sleep at night, huh? Plus, tomorrow's school! If you whine at 6AM, that you want to sleep more, then no one will be worse than me." She spoke. "No, I won't, mom." Asher sighed. He was going back upstairs when he heard the doorbell. "Can you see who it is, Asher?" Mrs. Hayes asked. "Sure." Asher turned around, and walked to the door. *It couldn't be Hope, could it? If it is, she'll be so mad at me! I don't even remember what I said to her,* Asher thought.

He swung the door open. Instead of an angry Hope, he saw two boys, grinning. One of the boys' hands were clutching a ball. "Hey, Josh. Hey, Evan. What do you have there?" Asher smiled, nervously.

"Asher, remember a girl named Hope--sorry, Hoppy?" Evan's grin widened. He passed the ball to his other hand and repeated.

"What about her?" Asher gulped.

"Come with us." Josh's hand hit Asher's back. He started to push him out of his house, out into the cold air. They crossed the street, heading toward the garden.

"You see, she's not the best girl and we've tried to tell you that before. You're lucky that we still keep in touch with you even after you keep calling her your 'friend'. Anyway, Amber told us that you went to that stupid book sale with your Hoppy."

"So what if I did?" Asher straightened his posture.

"See, Asher. You know that we really hate Hope, right?"

"Yeah. I know that." Asher sighed.

"Exactly. You see, we really don't want you to hang out with the likes of her, okay. She isn't cool at all nor is she popular. You know about the reputation we have in school and the town. If any of our friends are seen hanging out with non-cool, unpopular people, it hurts our reputation a lot. You get what we're saying, right?" Evan said.

Asher stopped in his tracks, "Are you guys saying that I shouldn't be friends with Hope?"

"You are smart!" Josh smiled. They led Asher to an area away from the benches, more toward the center of the garden. The grass was lush green but you couldn't really tell that anyway because of the darkness the clouds caused by covering the sun.

"Anyway, we got a ball so that we could play dodge ball. It'll help you realize how to dodge that Hoppy of yours." Evan rolled his eyes. He threw the ball in Asher's direction.

"Ha. You're joking, right? I would never stop being Hope's friend because two idiots told me to."

"What did you just call us, Hayes?"

"Let's just say that I would rather have Hope as my only friend than being friends with you guys." Asher slipped away. He escaped the garden where Josh and Evan brought him.

Asher was frantically going home when he saw someone at the door, about to ring the doorbell. It was Hope. "Hoppy!" Asher ran to her. She turned around, her face red. She was furious. "Where were you?! I've been calling your cell and you haven't been picking up." Hope demanded. Asher turned around, seeing Josh and Evan walking towards them. "Um, now's not a good time." Asher hesitated. "I don't care." Hope furrowed her eyebrows. Asher looked back again. Josh and Evan were getting closer. "Fine!" Asher opened the door and shoved himself and Hope inside. He locked the door, and took Hope to his room. "Mom, if Josh and Evan are at the door, do not answer!" Asher instructed.

"Sure. Why?" Mrs. Hayes. "I'll tell you later." He replied. Hope sat on Asher's bed.

"Look, Hoppy. When I hung up on you, my mom called me! She used my middle name, I got scared!" Asher started to explain, "I was going to call you back, but then Josh and Evan came and dragged me to the garden and started to tell me that I shouldn't be friends with you because you're not cool! I said no and that I will be your friend!" Hope looked surprised. "Wow. That's a lot. I came because Amber was just at my house." "What?!" Asher's eyes narrowed. He didn't expect to hear that from Hope.

"Yeah. She came wearing her ridiculous pink mini-skirt, fuzzy pink jacket and her 'I'm so cool' pink sunglasses." Hope mocked.

Asher snorted.

"Don't laugh! She came to my door, looked at me, moving her eyes up and down and said 'you know, I was right. You dress the same way you act: like a baby.' I wanted to pour bleach on her skin!" Hope complained, "Like, what's wrong with what I'm wearing?! It's literally just jeans and a shirt!"

"You look fine to me. I think it's just that she wears expensive, pink and—may I add—stupid clothes." Asher scoffed. Hope rolled her eyes. "I'm just tired of her! She deserves a punishment of some sort but I don't want to hurt her. I'd feel bad."

Asher laughed at that, "Hope, no offense but you are the only person on this planet who would feel bad about hurting someone who hurt you in the worst ways possible."

"I know! That's the problem!" Hope covered her face with her hands.

"Hey, it's okay! If you don't want to murder her yourself, I'm ready to do it! No charge." Asher said. Hope laughed, "Asher, what would I do without you?" "I don't know. I do know you would be helpless." Asher joked.

Hope hugged him.

"Hope. I understand what you are feeling right now, but I beg you, please let go." Asher stiffened. Hope let go. She smiled at him, her hazel eyes staring at his brown eyes. Asher smiled back at her. Hope sighed, "I just don't know what to do now."

"You know, if I were you, I'd forget everything and watch a Pixar movie. Specifically Inside Out or Coco." Asher smirked.

"Ash, it's 6PM. I'm not watching Inside Out or Coco right now. Besides, I'm 15. I have no interest in watching children's movies." Hope scoffed.

Asher raised his brows and widened his eyes. He was giving her an expression which said, 'Oh *really*?' It made Hope rolled her eyes.

"Why did Amber come to your house, anyway?" Asher asked.

"I don't know. She came, called me out on my outfit and asked about the cookies. I said they were definitely something unexpected. After I said that, she kinda just looked at me weird." Hope shrugged.

"Well, let's forget about Amber for now. Let's just talk." Asher sat down next to Hope.

"Yeah, okay. Let's talk about that whole conversation between Josh and Evan you just had." Hope straightened her back.

"Ugh. I already told you, they asked—no, *forced* me to not be friends with you and I said no." Asher rolled his eyes. "No? Is that all you said, 'no'? Because, seeing your expression when you came from there, it didn't seem like you said 'no' to them." Hope raised her brows.

Asher made eye contact with Hope until his eyes started to burn from staring at her pupil. "Fine. I said that I would rather give up being their friend than letting you go."

"Really?" Hope's eyes widened.

"Of course. You're a real friend, Hope." Asher smiled.

"Thanks, Asher." Hope smiled.

CHAPTER V

Young souls live dangerously

The next day, Hope and Asher met in the park after school. Hope got there early. She sat on a green bench, near the gate. She didn't see Asher anywhere near the gate and started getting anxious, *what if he isn't coming at all? What if he just told me to come here, to test my foolishness? Or what if--never mind. He's right there.* She saw him entering the park, his hands in his pockets, his black hair sticking to the back of his neck because of his sweat. Hope stood up and went to Asher. He was looking around, searching for Hope. She crept behind him and said, "Looking for someone?" Asher gasped and turned around. "You scared the crap out of me!" He smiled, his eyes widening. "I know." Hope chuckled. "Ha-Ha." Asher teased. "What took you so long?" Hope asked. "Mom asked me if I wanted some tea before coming here, so I've just had tea with milk." Asher sighed. "Thoughts?" Hope raised her eyebrows. "Disgusting." Asher scoffed, "I prefer water." Hope laughed. A roar of thunder came. "Looks like it'll rain any minute." Hope said, looking up at the blue sky covered by dark clouds. "I haven't gotten an umbrella. Looks like we're just going to be drenched." Asher grinned, his hair bouncing as he turned his gaze from the sky to Hope. "No! I've worn socks!" Hope groaned. "Too bad." Asher teased.

"Indeed, too bad." A voice came from behind them. It was Josh. "Asher, we talked about this, didn't we?"

"About the weather?"

"Haha. No. About you and your little friend here. We told you to not hangout with her."

"But, since you're here anyway, let's all play a game, shall we?"

"Which one?"

"Truth or dare. Sit." Josh and Evan sat down on the grass. Asher and Hope sat down as well.

"Well, well, well. Looks like I wasn't invited to your guys' little get together. I kinda feel like Maleficent now. Just way prettier." Amber walked up to them.

"Sit, Amber." Josh said.

"What are we playing?"

"Truth or dare."

"Hope, you go first." Evan smirked.

"She's here? Great." Amber rolled her eyes.

"Um...dare." Hope hesitated.

"That's what I wanted to hear. I dare you to go into that old library that was closed and get something from there, without help." Josh dared. Hope's eyes widened. *What the hell?!*

"What the hell, Josh?! That's literally illegal!" Asher raged.

"It's a dare." Josh smiled. They all got up. "Hoppy, you don't have to do this." Asher denied. "It's a dare, Asher." Amber teased. Hope didn't say anything. They all followed her to the library.

Hope looked at everyone, before entering the library. The door was locked. There was caution tape and a 'Do Not Enter' sign outside, and a huge lock on the door. She looked at everyone, "It's locked." "Oh for heaven's sake!" Amber came over, pulled a bobby pin from her hair and unlocked the lock with it. Hope took a few steps in, seeing nothing but some empty bookshelves. *What's even here to bring out, anyway?* She went further in, hoping to see something. *There.* She saw a small picture in which Liam

Colston was standing in front of the library, crossing his arms, grinning. It was dated back to 2006. *Perfect*. She went to it and reached her hand out to grab it but, she felt a grip on her arm, stopping her from taking it. She tried pulling her hand back but she couldn't. "What the--" She then felt herself being thrown to the floor. She fell. High pitched laughs surrounded her. "Who's there?!" Hope got up. A gust of wind passed through her, knocking her down again. "Who are you?" Hope asked, her voice trembling and her hands shaking. "**Don't come back.**" A child's voice whispered harshly. "What--" Hope was now being dragged by something she couldn't even see to the staircase which was in the foyer.

Outside, Asher was getting worried as the time passed. He was pacing, counting the seconds which passed. He reached 301 seconds and checked for Hope. Nobody was coming out. "She hasn't come yet. I'm going in." He announced. "Asher, she probably just hasn't found anything yet." Amber replied. "I don't care. Haven't you heard about the things which have happened in that library? I'm going in there." He ran to the library, sweating. He entered only to see Hope being dragged by her right leg to the top of the staircase by...nothing. "What the actual hell?" Asher gulped. "Ash! Help me, please!" Hope shrieked. He ran to her, not one thought running his mind. "Let go of her you...you--!" Asher hesitated. "Child!" Hope interrupted. Asher held Hope's arms, pulling her to where he was standing. "**Stop,**" The child mumbled. "You stop!" Hope cried. Asher pulled her to him. "Are you okay?" He asked. "I think." She responded. They both quickly ran out of the library.

"So, what have you gotten as a souvenir for us?" Josh asked.

"Trauma and confusion." Asher replied.

"Ha-Ha." Evan spoke.

"You spent ages in there. You have to have gotten something." Josh insisted.

"There was a literal child in there, attacking Hope!" Asher trembled.

Josh, Evan and Amber looked and each other and laughed.

"Asher, we know you didn't want Hope to go in there but you should've thought of a better excuse." Amber giggled.

"He isn't lying!" Hope hyperventilated. "There was a child's voice in there!"

"Hope, you really expect us to believe that there was a baby in there who *attacked* you?" Evan smirked.

"You both are horrible at this game. I think we'll have to compensate tomorrow. Okay? Meet us in the park, 5PM tomorrow." Josh threatened. He took Amber and Evan with him, leaving Hope and Asher alone.

CHAPTER VI

Asher's turn

"You did what?!" Mr. Eldrod fumed. "Dad--" "No! You broke into the library and was even thinking of stealing something! That's two crimes in less than 20 minutes, Hope! I've raised you to be better than this. You are lucky that Asher came in to save you from that...that thing!" "Mr. Eldrod, please don't scold Hope. If there's anyone to blame, it's me. I'm the reason Hope had to go in there." Asher interrupted. "That's also a problem, Asher! You both went for a walk, correct? How does breaking and entering along with stealing count as a 'walk'?! Based off of what you both have told us; you both could have died in there! They've closed that library for a reason!" Mr. Hayes snapped.

Hope and Asher sat on Hope's couch as they heard their fathers screaming at them, furiously. "Paul, David, I think you both should cool down for a few minutes. Martha and I'll talk to the kids." Mrs. Eldrod said. "You better not tell them that everything's okay, Ellie." Mr. Eldrod waved his finger at Mrs. Eldrod as he took Mr. Hayes to the kitchen. "Don't worry, sweeties. Your fathers are happy you both are alive. They just have a funny way of showing it." Mrs. Eldrod put her right hand on Hope's shoulder and the other on Asher's. "Exactly. We both are mad at you both too, it's just that we understand why you both did what you both did." Mrs. Hayes added. Hope and Asher smiled as their mothers went to talk to their fathers.

"I'm sorry, Ash."

"What for?"

"I'm the reason you had to come into the library. Because of me, we both are criminals." Hope covered her face with her hands. Asher looked at Hope, realizing how horrible she really feels. "Don't sweat it, Hoppy. In fact, I should be saying sorry. I'm the reason you had to go in there in the first place." He put his hand on her shoulder. "No. Stop trying to make yourself the bad guy. I was the one who didn't listen to you when I should've. I let Josh and Evan's words get to me. I've never fallen into peer pressure like this before!" Hope spoke. She was on the urge of tears. "Hey, Hoppy, look at me. You didn't do anything wrong, okay. If there's anyone to blame, it's Josh and Evan. They're the reason we both got wound up into a movie we didn't audition for." Asher reassured. He looked into Hope's eyes, now filled with tears, rolling down her cheek as she blinked. "Don't cry." Asher commanded. Hope wiped her tears away and looked at their parents. They were having a quiet, heated argument. Mr. Eldrod and Mr. Hayes sighed. They all came over to Hope and Asher, "Kids, all we're trying to say is that you really shouldn't have done that. You could've been arrested. If you both can realize that, we're fine with it. Just don't do it, regardless of who's telling you to." Mr. Eldrod stated. "We understand that at this age, peer pressure isn't something that you can escape. There are other kids who intimidate you and that's not a good thing." Mr. Hayes added. "Thanks, dad." Hope and Asher said in unison. "Just know, if there's anything you guys want us to do about those brats, just tell us, okay?" Mr. Eldrod said. "Dad, whatever you do, please don't say anything to them." Hope sighed. "Why not?" "Then, they'll just make our life an actual living hell." Asher looked down. "Oh, really?" Mrs. Hayes raised her eyebrows. "Don't worry, we won't say anything."

***

The next day, Asher came over to Hope's house before they went to the park to meet Josh, Evan and Amber. "Asher, I have an idea. Let's not go to the park today." Hope said. "Hope, if we don't go, Josh, Evan and Amber will come to our houses to get us. It's better if we go ourselves." Asher shook his head. Hope groaned at this. "Come on." Asher waved. "Okay, but wait. I need to pack a bag." Hope said. "Of what?" "Essentials for just in case they kidnap us." Hope answered, stuffing a bag with torches, batteries, a power bank and water bottles. "Hope, you're mad. You don't need to pack a bag." Asher said. "Yes, I do. I can imagine them giving us anesthesia and putting us in a van." Once she packed the bag, she followed Asher. "Mom, we're going to the park." Hope called. "Now, hold on a minute there, Hope. How will I know if you're in that library or not? No. If you're going anywhere, you're going to have to switch on your GPS tracker. If I feel like I need to, I will check your location and if I want to, I will call you--whenever I want-- and you have to pick up my call no matter what. If you don't, I will assume that you both are in jail, okay?" Mrs. Eldrod came over to the door, where Hope and Asher were standing. "Yes, Mom." Hope sighed. They both left, scared. "You don't think anything bad's gonna happen, do you?" Asher asked. "I hope not." Hope said, which made Asher snort. "You *hope* not, Hope?" He laughed. "You have the humor of an 11-year-old-boy." Hope rolled her eyes. "Come on, it was funny!"

"Look who's arrived...six minutes late!" Josh grinned. "Hello to you too, Josh." Asher rolled his eyes. "Alright, now. Asher, it's your turn. Truth or Dare?" Josh said. "Truth." Asher sighed. "Aw man. Not what I wanted. Anyway, tell us, what was the thing that you both saw yesterday in the library?"

"We didn't see anything." Asher answered.

"You didn't?"

"Nope. We only heard and felt it. It was some child's voice. It was too high-pitched to figure out if it was a girl or boy. Whatever it was, it literally picked Hope's leg up and started pulling her up the staircase."

"It did? How about we all come with you into the library and you can show us what it was and where it was." Evan suggested.

"Do we have to? I'm wearing my high high-heels." Amber scoffed.

"Yep. If you don't want to come, go home." Josh answered. Amber scoffed again. "Lead the way, Asher." Evan smiled. They all walked towards the library, when Hope remembered about what her mother told her. She quickly took her phone out of her pocket and turned off her location tracker. She switched her phone off and hid it back in her pocket. Once they made it to the library, they didn't see the lock on the door. "Nobody must've come to the library since yesterday." Asher assumed. They all crept inside, taking each step into the library very carefully. The high ceiling was adorned with ornate moldings and a large, tarnished chandelier that once cast a warm glow but now hung silently, collecting dust. The walls were lined with towering, empty bookshelves, their once-polished wood now faded and worn. In the center of the foyer stood the same grand, sweeping staircase made of dark wood, to which Hope was dragged. The steps creaked softly underfoot, a reminder of the many visitors who once climbed them in search of knowledge. The staircase split halfway up, leading to a balcony that overlooks the main floor, providing a vantage point of the vast, now eerily silent room. Tall, arched windows line the walls, their glass panes slightly fogged and cracked in places, allowing muted beams of light to filter through and cast long, ghostly shadows across the floor. The air was cool and still, carrying the faint, musty scent of aged paper and wood. A few scattered pieces of furniture, including worn reading tables and mismatched chairs, dotted throughout, adding to the sense of abandonment and faded elegance.

"Woah," Evan breathed.

"It's pretty once you have the time to look at it." Hope added.

"It is," Asher agreed.

"Can you guys just show us whatever that thing was so that we can get out of here?" Amber whined.

"Again, Amber, you can leave if you want." Josh said.

"Ow!" Evan shrieked.

"What happened?" Asher asked, turning to him.

"I felt someone slap the back of my head." Evan replied.

"There's no one behind you, bro." Josh chuckled.

"I know! That's what's--"

"OW!" Amber screamed, "Something's pulling my hair!"

Asher felt someone's grip tighten on his arm. He thought it was Hope, so, he looked in the direction of where he felt the person. Nobody was there. Somebody was still pulling Amber's long hair, so, Asher realized that there wasn't just one voice in this library. He held the part of his arm where he felt a grip. Instead of feeling his own skin, he felt a small hand which seemed to be made of clouds. He couldn't feel anything but dense air which felt like it was carved into the shape of a child's hand. "What the--" The lights went out. Candles burned out. Hope took out a torch and her phone. "I have no service. We can't contact anyone." She stated. "Is it just me, or did it get really cold in here all of a sudden?" Josh rubbed his hands together, his teeth chattering.

Asher felt the grip let go, tightening on his leg instead. It pulled him off the ground, making him grunt. "Asher?" Evan whispered, watching Asher being dragged to the center of the library by something which no one could see. "HOPPY!" Asher shrieked. Hope ran towards him, grabbing his arm to pull him to her. "Well, don't just stand there, help me!" Hope shouted to Josh, Evan and Amber. Josh and Evan ran to them, grabbing Asher's other arm. Amber slowly walked towards them, pulling Asher as well. They each pulled him with all their might, in hope of making the voice let go. "**Stop**," It said. "You stop! Let go of him!" Hope screamed. "Fine." It let go of Asher, "Listen, you're not supposed to be here. If you stay here for too long, she'll make you work." It spoke. "What? Who? Who'll make us work?" "She will." "Who's she?!" They all screamed in unison. "Look, I really want to tell you, I do, but she'll come and take me if I do. Just get out before she comes!" "Wait! How do we know if she's coming or not?!" Hope stood up, stopping the gust of wind that came from the voice. "You'll hear a little girl laughing, crying, and if she's really close, singing. She hasn't been seen by anyone but Nigel." "Who's Nigel?" Josh asked, his furrowed eyebrow deepening. "Exactly." It spoke. Everyone felt it leave the scene, all of them absolutely befuddled. Asher slowly got up. "Well, now what?" Evan huffed. "What do you mean 'now what'? Now, we go home!" Hope shouted. They were just about to leave, "Shhh! Do you hear that?" Amber whispered. Everyone heard a faint voice singing 'Jack and Jill went up the hill'. "That voice said that if 'she' is close, we'll hear a little girl singing..." Asher trailed off, his hands shaking. "We need to get out of here!" Amber whispered, harshly. "Too late." Hope said, looking at a shadow of a little girl growing taller and taller on the ground.

CHAPTER VII

Sirens

After Hope and Asher left, Mrs. Eldrod waited for Mr. Eldrod to get back home from work. She was making Mac and Cheese for dinner. She had kept the pasta to boil while she prepared the roux. She left the stove on as she heard the doorbell ring. Mrs. Eldrod washed her hands and opened it. "Hello, dear!" Mrs. Eldrod hugged Mr. Eldrod as he came inside the house from work. "Where's Hope?" He asked. "She and Asher have gone to the park." "Oh, really?" "Yes. Speaking of Hope, it's been 20 minutes since they left. I should check her location. She walked to the kitchen counter to get her phone. She opened the 'Find My Phone' app and checked Hope's location. "She's in the park--wait, what?" "What is it?" Mr. Eldrod hung his coat on the coat hanger. "It was just saying that she was in the park but then it showed 'Error'." "That only happens we you switch off your location, doesn't it?" "Yeah. Hold on, I'm calling her." The phone rang and went straight to voicemail. "Hello, it's Hope! You know the drill." It spoke. "I'll call Asher." Mr. Eldrod whipped out his phone and called Asher. "Sup, it's Asher. Leave a message after the beep."

"Why aren't either of them answering?" Mr. Eldrod furrowed his eyebrows.

"David, I'm getting scared. I told them that if they didn't answer, I'd assume they're in jail."

"No, don't worry. They're alright." Mr. Eldrod hugged Mrs. Eldrod and called Mr. Hayes.

"Hello? David?"

"Hey, Paul. Hope and Asher have gone to the park and Ellie told Hope to keep her tracker on so that she could check Hope's location but we've just checked and it's shown an error. We've called both the kids and neither of them are answering."

"What!? Hold on, I'll tell Martha to check Asher's location. I'm in the car right now."

"Yeah, okay." Mr. Eldrod hung up. Mrs. Eldrod smelled something burning. She turned around and realized the roux was burning. She rushed over and switched off the stove. "Hello?" She heard Mr. Eldrod say.

"Okay, so, Martha checked and she's saying that Asher's location's off. I'm turning around and going to the park. Martha's coming, too."

"Alright, we'll be there." He hung up and said, "Come, Ellie. Paul and Martha are going to the park to find Hope and Asher."

"Okay..." Mrs. Eldrod ran her hands through her hair. They went outside and walked to the park. "You don't think Hope and Asher got arrested, do you?" Mrs. Eldrod asked. "Ellie, don't worry. Hope and Asher are smart kids. I'm sure they're fine." Mr. Eldrod trembled as he put his arm around Mrs. Eldrod. "David, who are you trying to convince, me or yourself?" "Both."

Once they got there, Mr. Hayes waved to them. They waved back and rushed over to the Hayes'. "Have you seen them?" "No. We've been looking for them for a couple of minutes, now." Mrs. Hayes said. "Let's keep looking. Maybe they're nearby."

They looked for about 30 minutes with no luck. "That's it. I think we should call the police." Mrs. Hayes sighed. "Yeah, I think we should." Mrs. Eldrod agreed. "I'll dial the number right now." Mr. Hayes called 911.

"Hello? Yes, I'm Paul Hayes. My son, Asher Hayes and his friend, Hope Eldrod, had gone to the park about 45 minutes ago and we told them to keep their location tracker on but it's not and neither of them are answering our calls. They're not in the park and we're getting really worried."

"Alright, send we've tracked your location. Officers will be there in about 10 minutes."

"Thank you." Mr. Hayes said. "They're coming."

"Well, what do we do until then?" Mr. Eldrod asked.

"I guess we just stand here and keep checking their locations." Mrs. Eldrod replied.

***

Everyone heard sirens once the police arrived. 'Oh, good god! They're here.' Mrs. Eldrod gulped, realizing that this was real. All of these sirens made her feel dizzy. Never in her life had she thought that her daughter would become a criminal and go missing, let alone all in the same week.

"Alright, can someone please tell me when was the last time you saw these two?" Officer Runt emerged from the white vehicle, getting a notepad out from the dashboard.

"Yes, sir. They were last seen at 5PM. They both were coming this park. We've already checked the park and the nearby streets," Mr. Eldrod said, his voice strained. "There's no sign of them."

Officer Runt nodded, taking notes. "We'll organize a search party immediately. Time is crucial in these situations. We just need a photograph of each child. The sooner we get it, the better. I'd prefer a hardcopy."

"Yes, officer." Mrs. Hayes came over, her voice trembling. She held a photograph of Hope and Asher sitting together, laughing. "Will this do?" She asked, tears running down her cheeks. "Yes, ma'am. Don't worry, we will do our best to make sure the kids are back home, safe and sound."

As the officers spread out to search the neighborhood, the parents huddled together, their fear and helplessness growing with each passing minute. Mrs. Eldrod tried to stay strong, but the tears flowed freely as she imagined Hope and Asher, lost and scared. Mr. Eldrod wrapped his arms around her, offering what little comfort he could. While they sat there, they saw a woman wearing a large fur coat. She had short hair and was wearing extremely large sunglasses. She was running towards them. "Amber, my baby! Where are you?!" She started shouting. "Ma'am? What are you doing?" Officer Runt came over to her. "My little girl, Amber! She came to the park an hour ago but now that it's time for dinner, my nanny just called and said that Amber wasn't answering any of her calls or texts."

"Curiouser and curiouser. Another missing child report. Do you know if there any other kids with Amber?"

"Her best friend, Josh and I think his friend Evan also came." Amber's mom said.

"Alright. Do any of you have Josh or Evan's parents' contact?" Officer Runt asked.

"I have Josh's." Amber's mom replied. She called Josh's mom and told her to come to the park with Evan's parents, too.

"Alright, with situations like this, it's probably just the teenage immaturity that led them to wander off somewhere. I'm sure we'll find them momentarily." Officer Runt assured.

"Officer, I really hope you're right." Mrs. Eldrod's voice was breaking. She was shaking her leg, holding Mrs. Hayes' hand as they both cried silently.

"Wait, you're Hope's mother, right? Has Hope gone missing too?" Amber's mom looked at Mrs. Eldrod.

"Yes! And I'm sure that it's because of your daughter!"

"My daughter? But she's gone missing too! How is she the problem?"

"Kelly, your daughter keeps bullying my daughter! She calls her 'Joke' instead of 'Hope', says she acts like a baby, and she says her freckles look like a connect-the-dots puzzle!" Mrs. Eldrod fumed.

"What? I-I-I'm sorry. I didn't know..."

"Well, sorry doesn't fix things, does it? Now, our children are lost and it's your daughters' fault!" Mrs. Hayes stood up.

CHAPTER VIII

Only one spoon

"Indeed, too late." A little girl's voice said, "I do hope I didn't interrupt anything, did I? Nobody was here, right?" Everyone looked at each other and then turned their gaze back to the circle of wind from which the voice was coming. "There was?" It spoke. "Well, that is a shame. I wanted to introduce myself to you guys! But I can still do that. I'm Fedora Blinkan. I died when I was 4 years old. Give me a second." It stopped talking and suddenly, the wind passed right through them all, making them shiver. "Now, look at me." It spoke. When they looked, instead of a circle of wind, they saw a little girl who was covered in blood. Head to toe, bloody. She grinned, showing her bloodstained teeth. Hope, Asher, Josh and Evan audibly gasped; Amber shrieked. She ran to the door and started pulling it with all her might. "It won't work. I've tried it too." Fedora said. "What?" Amber looked back at Fedora, and then her hands. They were all bloody. "What the hell?!" "I know." Fedora came over to Amber and held her hands. "These soft hands are covered with blood. Just like mine. Although, your hands are covered in my blood. Mine are too, just a bit more brutally than yours." "I'm sorry, if you died at four, and you're a ghost, how are you able to talk in English so fluently?" Hope gulped.

"I live in a library! You hear people talk in strong English all the time! I've only just died at four. That was 4 years ago! I'm technically 8 years old now."

"Wait, if you died 4 years ago, why are you haunting people now?" Evan asked.

"That's the question, isn't it?" Fedora went from Amber to Evan. "I've been feeling something, lately. I've been feeling a strange presence which repeatedly awakens my spirit. It doesn't let my soul get its peace. I need to find it before it haunts me forever. But I can't find what it is until I've found out how I died."

"How does that have anything to do with this?"

"It does! I get an awful feeling from that presence. My guardian thinks it's my murderer. That's why she keeps sending me down here! I must find out who murdered me and how they murdered me in order to bring them to my guardian."

"So, you need to kill them?" Josh straightforwardly asked.

"Yes." Fedora sighed. "And you all are going to help me do that. I've found six out of ten clues to find out who my killer is. You all can help me find the last four."

"Do we have to?" Asher asked, irritated.

"Yes. You all are trapped here until you complete my challenges to get the clues. There is a twist, though. If either one of you gets possessed by a ghost during a challenge, another challenge will be given to free whoever gets possessed. So, be careful. If you aren't able to save the person who gets possessed, they'll be forever reserved in this book, with the rest of my former prisoners." She pointed to a book with hundreds of pages. "You'll have 30 minutes to complete your first task. You must the item using the riddle my guardian gave me. It is: 'Be stabbed by me and it will not hurt. There are different ways to get me killing. All the killers love me most. You'll find me in a place where not many people roam.' Your time starts...now!"

"Oh god!" Hope exclaimed. "What in the world does she mean by that?"

"I think we need to find the item that the riddle is describing." Amber suggested.

"Thank you, Captain Obvious!" Evan yelled, "If it says 'Be stabbed by me and it will not hurt, then it has to be talking about a knife or a dagger. You can't be stabbed by a sword and not have it hurt. Plus, it said 'There are different ways to get me killing,' so that must mean that it can be thrown or slid to someone."

"You're right! Quick, everyone start looking for a knife or a dagger in a place where not a lot of people go!" Josh said.

"Wait, first, take these torches. It'll be easier." Hope handed everyone a torch.

"Thanks, Hope!" Asher smiled.

"Think, guys! Where's a place where not a lot of people go?"

"Is there a room which is only allotted to the staff, maybe?"

"I'll go check!" Josh ran to the back of the library, hoping to see something. He walked along the wooden bookshelves, moving his hand along them as he walked. As he was going, he saw a door with a sign on, reading 'NO ENTRY. STAFF ONLY.' He looked around, and snuck inside. He looked around, seeing nothing but a few rats, and a few rags lying around. There were a few chairs stacked up in one corner, and two tables put off to the side. 'It'd be pretty sad if the so called 'staff' had to each lunch in here.' Josh started to pick up all the rags lying on the ground, in hope of seeing a dagger beneath one of them. While he was, he heard a gust of wind enter the room. At first, he didn't think much of it, but as a few minutes went by, he felt the air getting denser and colder. He heard the winds shifting as he searched for the weapon.

***

"What's taking Josh so long?" Evan said, irritated.

They heard a scream from the back of the library.

"Who did that?!" Amber clung to the bookshelf.

"I don't--woah." Asher stopped. He saw Josh's shadow growing taller and taller. They saw Josh standing in front of them, only, something was different about him. His eyes weren't as brown as they usually were. In fact, they were gray. Although, no one could see his eyes. The torches only shone so much light.

"Oh no! Someone's been possessed!" Fedora whispered, harshly. "Figure out who it is and I'll tell you how to save them."

"Josh... what do you have there?" Evan asked.

"Hm? This? Nothing." Josh's voice was different. He was more low-pitched than usual.

"It's Josh. He's possessed."

"Correct! Maybe next time you won't leave your friends alone?" Fedora grinned, her bloodstained teeth sticking out. "Now, to save him, you all will have to eat one spoonful of salt, each. Failure to do so will cause him to be reserved into that book."

"WHAT?!" Amber cried. "A SPOONFUL OF SALT?!"

"Correct."

"Amber, just do it, or else he'll die!" Evan pleaded.

"Here," Fedora pointed towards a table which suddenly had 4 spoons, and a jar of salt sitting on it. "Line up."

They lined up, each of them preparing to do something disgusting. Hope went first. She picked the spoon up, scooped salt into it and rushed it into her mouth. As soon as the salt touched her tongue, a wave of shock coursed through her. The intense, overwhelming taste made her eyes water and her face contort in an involuntary grimace.

She felt a burning sensation in her throat, and her stomach churned in protest. The saltiness was so overpowering that it seemed to drown out every other sensation, leaving her momentarily disoriented. She quickly reached for her bag to get her water bottle, desperate to wash away the lingering, abrasive taste. After her; Evan, Asher, and Amber ate the salt.

"Very good! Release him, Theodore." Fedora said, in a more disappointed tone than congratulative. Suddenly, Josh fell to the floor, blood rushing back into his cheeks. He sat up, coughing violently. "Josh! Are you okay?" Evan ran to him. "I'm fine. Here, I found the dagger." Josh handed the dagger to Hope. She then placed it on the table for Fedora to grab.

"Wonderful work, everyone! Now, it's time for your next task."

CHAPTER IX

Nobody's necklace

"What do we need to find now?" Amber groaned. "The front of me is the source of a song. Or to kiss with a fervor of love lifelong. My back is a plant fit for a queen, crafted by needle, chemical, or machine. You'll find me in a place where, to get around in a shopping mall, you might use an elevator, or you might walk up and down what's like a non-moving escalator. You guys have 30 minutes to find it. Go!"

"Alright, so we can't split up because the last time we split up, Josh got possessed. We'll have to go in pairs. Think: to get around in a shopping mall, you might use an elevator, or you might walk up and down what's like a non-moving escalator.... it's the staircase! A staircase is a non-moving escalator!" Asher said.

"Yeah, but you're not focusing on the main riddle. 'The front of me is the source of a song. Or to kiss with a fervor of love lifelong. My back is a plant fit for a queen, crafted by needle, chemical, or machine'." Hope pointed out.

"It's obvious, isn't it?" Amber stepped in. "It's a necklace. The front of me, (the first part of the word is neck) songs come from here and it also means to kiss. The second part of the word (my back) is lace. The first part is a reference to the flower, queen Anne's lace. The final line is a reference to all the different ways that lace is currently made."

"You know what, that might actually work." Hope raised her eyebrows.

"But why would a necklace be in the staircase?" Evan asked.

"If a dagger could be in the staffroom and a four-year-old ghost could be in a library, a necklace in a staircase wouldn't surprise me." Asher sighed.

"Okay, Let's go!"

"Wait! There are two staircases! The main one and the one back there." Josh pointed to where he went to find the dagger.

"Well then, Asher, Josh, and I can go to the main one and you guys can look at the back one." Evan suggested.

"Alright." Amber shrugged.

They ran to the staircase, checking for a necklace to be left on it. Amber caught a glimpse of Hope's eyes darting anxiously, scanning the floor. The panic in Hope's movements makes her chest tighten. She'd never seen Hope like this: vulnerable, desperate. And for once, Amber wanted to help, genuinely and without condition. When Hope glanced at her, she noticed there was a flicker of distrust. Amber swallowed hard, then crouched beside her, the creaking floorboards groaning beneath their weight.

"Hey, let's start over here," she suggested softly, pointing to a stair. The past slights and hurtful words seemed almost palpable between them, but Amber pushed through it. *She's more than what I did to her.* That thought drove her.

Hope kneeled beside her, trembling hands shoving aside debris and old, torn pages. Amber wanted to say something comforting, but the words felt clumsy. Instead, she picked up a broken glass shard and used it to sift through the mess more carefully. They worked side by side, the silence between them heavy, but different from the poisonous quiet of their past encounters. There was a shared purpose now.

A chill ripples through the air as a faint, ghostly whisper echoes through the empty aisles. Hope's breath hitches, eyes widening. Amber saw the fear gripping her, and she moved closer as she placed a steadying hand on Hope's shoulder.

"Hey, look at me." Hope's gaze snaps to her, confusion and wariness mixed with the terror. "We'll find it," Amber promises firmly. The spirits' presence thickens, their invisible eyes on the girls. Amber sensed the hatred stirring, the tension tightening around them like a knot. There was no time for more searching. Then Hope noticed a glint beneath a stair which was ripping off. Heart pounding, she reached out and pulled the necklace free—its delicate chain intact, the necklace still gleaming faintly. She held it out, rejoiced. Amber held her hand up, silently asking for a high-five.

For a moment, Hope's fingers hovered in front of Amber's. The hesitation stung, but Amber didn't retract her hand. She was determined to make amends, even if this small gesture didn't erase the years of pain. Hope finally clapped her hand, her fingers brushing Amber's in a fleeting touch. The tension shifts, just slightly. They ran down the staircase, "Asher, Josh, Evan! We found it!" Hope screamed.

"What?! How?" Fedora came to her. "That's impossible!"

"We found it, look!" Hope rejoiced. She kept it on the table.

Fedora snatched it from the table. "Where did you find this?

"There was one stair which was like ripping off. We tore the whole stair off and found it there." Amber said.

"Oh. I didn't think of that..." Fedora trailed off. Asher, Josh and Evan came running inside. "You guys found it?"

They asked. "Yeah!"

"Where was it?"

"It was inside a stair." Amber said.

"Really?"

"Hope found it." Amber said. Hope's eyebrows rose. This was the first time Amber hadn't taken credit for something Hope had done.

"Alright, well. Now that that's over with, we move on to your next object."

"But wait, how does a necklace have anything to do with getting revenge on your murderer?"

"This necklace is nobody's necklace. I was wearing this when he murdered me. He ripped it off of my neck as he..." Fedora's cheeks were now wet with tears and blood. "I need to show it to him in order to make sure he remembers it. Murderers who kill little children like the way he killed me don't really remember who they killed unless they are reminded."

"So, you need the necklace to remind him of your death?"

"No! I need to show it to him and rip it of his hands the way he ripped it off my neck."

CHAPTER X

Illicit dares

"Officer, have you found them?" Mrs. Eldrod got up, seeing Officer Runt walk to them.

"No, ma'am. Look, I need one last thing from you all. Do you know any place which the children may have gone to?" Officer Runt asked, panting. The Hayes and Eldrod looked at each other, hesitant. They all had an idea that the kids went to the library again, but that would've led their children to jail.

"Sir, yesterday," Mr. Eldrod began, "The kids were playing truth or dare and Josh told Hope to prove that she was a good friend by going into the closed library and getting something outside of it. Out of peer pressure, Hope went in and tried getting a photograph but, she couldn't because she said that something was pulling her leg and was dragging her up the staircase."

"Well, that is serious. People had reported paranormal activities, which was why we closed the place. We'll have a discussion about this later but for now, we need to check the library. They're kids; they might've gone there again."

The sun had set, and the streetlights cast long shadows across the quiet neighborhood. The officers, moved with determination, their flashlights cutting through the darkness. Their radios crackled with updates and instructions. Behind them, the parents of the missing children followed closely, their faces etched with worry and fear. Mrs. Eldrod clutched Mrs. Hayes hand tightly, as Mrs. Hayes did the same. When the officers reached the library doors, they tried to open them, but the doors wouldn't budge. Officer Runt signaled to his team, and they attempted to force the doors open, but they remained stubbornly closed. The creaking of the hinges echoed in the stillness, added to the tension of the moment.

Mrs. Eldrod, her voice trembling, asked, "What happened? Why aren't the doors opening?"

The Officer Runt turned to her; his expression serious. "The doors are stuck, ma'am. We're trying to get them open, but it's taking longer than expected." They kept trying to knock the door down, but it wouldn't budge.

Inside, the library was dark and filled with rows of towering bookshelves, but the officers couldn't get in. The parents stood close, their hearts pounding as they started to think of the worst. The scene was a mix of hope and fear, as everyone worked together, desperately trying to find a way inside to rescue the missing children.

Mrs. Eldrod fell to the ground, her hands trembling as she clutched a crumpled tissue. Beside her, Mrs. Hayes stared at the ground, her own grief etched deeply into her face. The library, usually a place of interest and happiness, now felt like a cruel reminder of their missing children.

Mrs. Eldrod's eyes were fixed on the doors where Hope and Asher entered. The sight of them made her heart ache. She couldn't shake the feeling of anger that simmered just beneath her sorrow. She blamed Amber's mother for everything. If only she had kept a closer watch on her daughter, maybe Hope and Asher would still be here. "I can't believe this is happening," Mrs. Eldrod whispered, her voice breaking. "How could she let this happen? Amber has always been trouble, and now... now Hope and Asher are gone."

Mrs. Hayes reached out, placing a comforting hand on Mrs. Eldrod's shoulder. "We'll find them," she said softly, though her own voice wavered with uncertainty. "We have to believe that."

The two mothers sat in silence, united in their grief and their desperate hope for their children's safe return. The park around them seemed to hold its breath, as if waiting for the moment when Hope and Asher would come running back, laughing and carefree. But for now, all they could do was wait and hope.

CHAPTER XI

Rare Ravens

"Alright, now. Your next object is, 'I have feathers that help me fly. When I was born, my eyes were bright blue. I can point in directions and puncture wood, how far I fly depends on you. I'm not low. I always fly high.' You'll have 15 minutes to find it." Fedora stated.

"15? Last time we got 30!" Evan argued.

"Yes, and last time you got the object within 10 minutes. I'm sure 15 minutes is good enough for you guys to find it. Go!" Fedora shooed them away.

"Alright, we don't have enough time. Think, 'I have feathers that help me fly. When I was born, my eyes were bright blue. I can point in directions and puncture wood, how far I fly depends on you. I'm not low. I always fly high.' Which bird has bright blue eyes when they're just born?" Hope said.

"Ravens! But, how would we find a raven in here?" Josh exclaimed.

"There must be a raven statue here. The riddle said, 'I'm not low. I always fly high.' So, the raven will have to be on somewhere on the next two floors." Asher said.

"Well then, let's get going!" Hope said. They rushed to the staircase and looked around the floor. Hope looked through a bookshelf, hoping to see a raven. It was empty, except for a few old cloths and cobwebs.

"Do you think anything related to ravens' counts?" Amber asked, blowing the dust off of a book.

"I wouldn't risk it. Let's get everything about ravens. One of them has got to be the answer." Asher suggested.

Asher walked around, arms at his sides. He scanned every corner of the library, searching. Determined, he began his search, weaving through the labyrinth of shelves. He scanned the titles, hoping for a clue. His fingers brushed against the spines of ancient tomes, leaving trails in the dust. He paused at a large, ornate desk in the center of the room, its surface cluttered with yellowed papers and broken quills.

Asher's eyes caught sight of a peculiar book; its cover adorned with a silver raven. He pulled it from the shelf, the weight of it surprising him. As he opened it, a small key fell out, clinking softly on the floor. He picked it up, his pulse quickening. The key had to be important.

He continued his search, now looking for a lock that the key might fit. "Anyone found anything, yet?" Hope shouted. "I found a key!" Asher looked around, for a while. "Guys, I can't seem to find the keyhole. Can you all help?" "Sure!" Hope said. Everyone started looking around for the keyhole. As they were, Amber felt something touch her. It felt like a small hand.

Asher found a small, hidden compartment behind a loose brick in the wall. With trembling hands, he inserted the key and turned it. The compartment opened to reveal the silver raven statue, gleaming even in the dim light.

Asher let out a breath he hadn't realized he was holding. He had found it. The statue was his. "Guys! I found it!" Asher exclaimed, "Guys?" He turned around and saw Amber floating in the air. "Amber?" He heard Hope whisper. They heard Amber grunting and screaming. She suddenly dropped to the ground and opened her eyes. They were gray and faded. She slowly got up and said, "Guys?" Her voice was high-pitched. She still held her flashlight, pointing it towards the others.

"Oh no! She's been possessed! You guys will have two minutes to help her. You must find four bananas and eat them all in under 10 seconds. You'll have two minutes to find and eat them. Go!" Fedora came and spoke.

"What?! You're basically just asking us to kill her! How are we supposed to find and eat four bananas in 2 minutes?!" Josh argued.

"Well, 1 minute and 15 seconds."

"Run!" Hope screamed. They all scattered in different directions, looking for the bananas. "Where the hell would there be bananas here?!" Evan shouted. "I don't know, but we'll have to find out quickly!" Asher replied, quickly. Hope's heart pounded as she navigated the dusty aisles. The dim light filtering through broken windows cast eerie shadows, making her jump at every creak and groan of the old building. She clutched her flashlight, its beam flickering. "Amber needs us," she whispered to herself, determination mingling with resentment. "Even if she was a bully, no one deserves this." Her mind raced with memories of Amber's taunts, but also of Josh's unwavering friendship with her. "No one can die tonight," she thought, scanning the shelves for the elusive bananas among the decaying books and cobwebs.

Asher's mind was a whirlwind of thoughts. He tried to stay calm, but the gravity of the situation weighed heavily on him. "We have to find those bananas," he muttered, pushing aside a stack of ancient tomes. His logical mind tried to piece together where they might be hidden. "Think, Asher, think. Where would someone hide bananas in a library?" He remembered Amber's sharp words and the way she treated Hope, but also Josh's loyalty to her. He moved methodically, checking every nook and cranny, his eyes sharp and focused.

Evan felt a mix of fear and guilt. He pushed through the fear, knowing he had to make things right. "Amber, hang in there," he whispered, his voice trembling. He rummaged through the debris, his hands shaking. Every shadow seemed to mock him, but he pushed on, driven by the need to save her. "We will find those bananas," he told himself, trying to believe it. "We have to."

Josh's mind was a storm of emotions. Anger at the situation, fear for Amber, and a fierce determination to save her. "We can't lose her," he thought, his jaw clenched. He moved quickly, almost recklessly, through the library, knocking over piles of books in his haste. "Bananas, where are you?" he growled under his breath. He thought of Amber's laughter, and how she always believed in him. "We won't let you down, Amber," he vowed, his eyes scanning the room with a fierce intensity. "We will save you."

Josh, Hope, Asher, and Evan knew they had to act quickly. Amber's life was slipping away, and the ghost inside her was growing more powerful. These bananas were the key to breaking the possession and saving Amber's life. The possession was a harrowing ordeal, pushing the group to their limits as they fought against time and the hostile force threatening their friend.

"You have 30 seconds left!" Fedora's voice entered their ears, painfully. She started counting down the seconds, pressurizing the four to work faster. "Where the hell are those bananas, Fedora?!" Josh screamed. He lost it. He started throwing things away, desperately trying to find the one thing that could save Amber.

"15, 14, 13, 12..." Fedora's voice echoed throughout the library.

"SHUT UP, FEDORA!" They fumed, tears filling their eyes. "10, 9, 8, 7..."

This is it.

"5, 4, 3..."

There's no hope left.

"2, 1!"

Amber suddenly fell to the floor. Fedora's hand, cold and ethereal, reached out and plunged into Amber's chest. She shuddered violently, her eyes wide with terror and pain. Her friends could only watch, paralyzed by fear, as the life drained from her body.

Amber's flashlight clattered to the floor, its beam casting a stark, unsteady light on her lifeless form. Fedora lingered for a moment, her merciless gaze sweeping over Asher, Hope, Evan, and Josh, as if warning them of their fate should they remain. Then, with a final, chilling wail, Fedora, left the friends in stunned silence, their hearts pounding with a mix of grief and terror. There was a pool of blood, growing bigger and bigger beneath Amber's body.

Hope ran to her, "Amber?" "Hope, I'm sorry. I didn't mean to hurt you. I was just...jealous." Amber whispered, before closing her eyes for the last time. "Amber!" Hope shrieked. Josh, Asher and Evan came to Hope's side. She shook her, slapped her and performed a brief CPR. Nothing worked. She checked Amber's pulse and panicked. "She's dead." She very slightly managed to slip out of her mouth, tears running down her cheeks.

CHAPTER XII

Old Hourglass

"I'm a mixture of minutes and sand. I have two halves, though both are joined in one. The more I stand still, the faster I run. I can be anywhere." Fedora's voice echoed.

"Fedora, Amber just died! Can you not be the insensitive little idiot you are?!" Josh screamed, crying.

"Oh, I'm sorry. I didn't realize it was my fault that you guys couldn't find four bananas." Fedora said.

Hope couldn't process what had just happened. She had just witnessed the murder of her bully; something she had always wished for. But now that it had happened, she couldn't help but blame herself for everything. If she hadn't accepted the dare yesterday, nothing like this would've happened. Life would've been normal. Amber would've been alive and ready to bully Hope again. She kept thinking about Amber's last words. 'Hope, I'm sorry. I didn't mean to hurt you. I was just...jealous.' Never in her life would Hope have thought that Amber was jealous of her. From which angle would Hope be worthy of being jealous of? She wasn't privileged, nor rich. She had nothing Amber did. That's probably why Amber was jealous of her, though. After all, we always want what we don't have.

"Now, if you guys take longer than 30 minutes to find the last object, I will kill you all." Fedora gladly threatened. "Fedora, just shut up. It's for the best." Asher trembled. "Asher, I think you'll need to get up and start searching, or you're going to end up just like her." Fedora came to Asher, making direct eye contact as she pointed at Amber's cold, dead body. He, Evan and Josh slowly got up. "Hope, come on."

"No."

"Hope, you don't have a choice."

"No. You guys find it. I can't."

"Alright. Suit yourself." Evan shrugged. They left, going away to find the object. Hope was all alone, with Amber's dead body. It was just a matter of days before Hope had said that she wanted to kill Amber, once and for all. Now, here she was, staring at her dead body. The pain bit into her skin, making it hard to breathe. She didn't know why she was sobbing. Amber had always been an awful person to Hope and the only thing Hope had wanted was for Amber to die. Now that it was done, Hope couldn't help but feel guilty. She hadn't wanted this to happen. Not like this. She stared at Amber's pale cheeks. Her soft hands, her hair and her words. 'You should put makeup, Joke.', 'You're such a crybaby, Joke.' The sentences stung her like a bee. She never expected this to happen. What will she tell her parents? How will Hope ever face them again? What will she say to Amber's mom? All these thoughts made Hope shiver and curl up into a ball. She looked at Amber and wiped a tear off her own cheek. Hope wiped off the small puddle of blood on Amber's forehead. She shook off the blood and sat in silence.

As she did, Asher, Josh and Evan were looking throughout the library, sad and tired. Josh hadn't processed what had happened, nor did Asher or Evan. They had figured out that the object was an hourglass because it was obvious. Nobody bothered to say anything. The death of Amber had taken such an unexpected hit on everyone. They kept looking, trying not to focus on anything else. That was when Asher realized that they had left Hope alone. Alone to get possessed and, eventually, die. He sprinted back to her and saw her staring at Amber's body. "Hoppy, come with me. You're not safe here, alone. You don't have to do anything. Just hold my hand." He held out his hand. She held it and got up. They both went back to where Josh and Evan were. "Where did you go?" Josh asked Asher, not looking away from where he was looking. "I went to get Hope. We couldn't risk her being all alone there, otherwise--" Asher began.

"She wasn't alone! Amber was there with her!"

"She's dead, Josh."

"No, she's not! She's going to get up and walk right towards us right now." Josh looked at them, eyes red and filled with tears. He was pointing towards her body, distant from them.

"Josh. She's gone. Forever." Hope whispered.

"No she's not!" Josh sobbed. He fell on his knees, every tear flowing like a river.

They heard something shift. "Psst!" They heard a little boy say. "What was that?!" Evan jumped. "Me." The boy said. They all felt something pass right through them and suddenly, they saw a young boy, no older than 6 years. "Hello. I'm Nigel. I saw what Fedora did to your friend, there. That isn't the first time someone's died here. All the ghosts here have died here. Except for Fedora." He spoke.

"What?" They all said in unison.

"Fedora's been looking for her murderer for a year, now. I had come here with my father the day I died. My father took a step away from me to look at a book and that's when I met her. She said she'd be my best friend. I believed her and followed her. My dad looked for me for hours, only to find my dead body on the third floor. Fedora asked me to look for the same hourglass you guys are looking for right now. I couldn't find it. I didn't even know what an hourglass was. Because of that, she killed me." Nigel explained. "She's not even here to kill her murderer as revenge. She just wants more ghosts here. She was the first one here and also the most powerful."

"So, we're just wasting our time here?" Hope asked, catching her breath.

"Kind of, yeah. I'll help you guys out. Here," He handed them the hourglass. "I've been looking for it ever since I died. She's been making me. I don't want you guys to die a young death the way I did. Take it and run. You only have 10 minutes left, now." Nigel disappeared.

Evan's eyes were wide open and his jaw dropped as he realized, "Guys, we're done. We're out of here now."

They ran downstairs and screamed in unison, "FEDORA!"

"What?"

"We found it."

"WHAT?! HOW IS THAT POSSIBLE?!" She stormed, snatching the hourglass from Evan's hands.

"We found it, now let us out." Josh trembled.

"Hmm? Oh, of course. You'll need to get out now...hold on."

"No! We want to leave now!" Asher ordered.

"Wait! You can't leave yet! We haven't gotten to know each other that well, Asher!" Fedora argued.

"Fedora, you have your objects. Now let us go!" Hope commanded.

"Wait! You cannot leave," Fedora's voice echoed through the room, a haunting whisper that seemed to come from everywhere and nowhere at once. "This place is my prison, and now it is yours."

Hope stepped forward, her voice trembling but determined. "We did everything you asked. We solved the puzzles, found the items. Why won't you let us go?"

Fedora's form wavered, and for a moment, it seemed as though she might relent. But then, her expression hardened. "You have done what was required, but you have not understood. This library holds more than just books and secrets. It holds my pain, my memories. Until you understand my story, you will remain."

Asher glanced at the others, his face pale. "What do we do now?" he whispered.

Josh clenched his fists, frustration evident in his eyes. "We need to find out what happened to her. It's the only way."

Evan nodded; his gaze fixed on Fedora. "We need to uncover her past, understand her suffering. Only then will she set us free."

"I remember the library as a place of wonder and adventure. My parents often brought me there, and I would lose myself in the colorful illustrations of the storybooks. One evening, as the sun dipped below the horizon, casting long shadows across the room, I wandered away from my parents, drawn to a corner filled with old, dusty books. I was flipping through the pages of a particularly large book when I heard the door creak open. A man entered; his face hidden in the dim light. He moved quietly, almost like a shadow himself. At first, I thought he was just another visitor, but something about him made me uneasy.

He approached me slowly, his eyes cold and devoid of kindness. I tried to back away, but my small legs couldn't move fast enough. He grabbed me, his grip tight and painful. I wanted to scream, but fear choked my voice. He whispered something I couldn't understand, his breath hot and foul against my ear. He ripped my necklace off of my neck.

In a swift, brutal motion, he ended my life. The pain was sharp and fleeting, and then everything went dark. My blood flew everywhere. My last thoughts were of my parents, of the stories I would never finish, and of the life I would never live. When I awoke, I was no longer a little girl but a ghost, bound to the library where my life had been so cruelly taken. I watched as my parents grieved; their hearts shattered by my loss. I wanted to reach out to them, to tell them I was still here, but I couldn't. I was trapped, a silent witness to their sorrow." Fedora explained.

"I-I'm so sorry, Fedora. But that still doesn't allow you to hold us hostage here." Hope said.

"I know! That's why I won't. I'm going to kill you all instead."

"What?!"

"You can't do that!"

"Oh, but I can! Come here!" She darted towards them, just barely missing.

Hope, Asher, Josh and Evan all ran as fast as they could towards the main entrance. Fedora hissed and followed them. They couldn't open the door in time so, they dashed towards the nearest window, which was up on the second floor. They hesitated at first, but then turned back to see Fedora coming for them. Evan smashed the glass and they all jumped out. As they were jumping out, Hope saw Fedora sprinting towards them. She picked up a chunk of glass and threw it at Fedora's face. Fedora's figure suddenly disintegrated. They jumped. It wasn't a life-threatening jump, thankfully. They all fell flat on their backs, creating a loud thud as they touched the ground. They could no longer see Fedora. "Hope, what did you do?" Josh asked. "I don't know. And I don't think we should find out."

CHAPTER XIII

Doors not yet open

The officers still hadn't opened the doors yet. It was 9PM now. Mr. and Mrs. Eldrod, Mr. and Mrs. Hayes, Amber's mom, Josh's mom and Evan's mom hadn't left the front of the library since what felt like forever.

The parents stood huddled together outside the crumbling facade of the abandoned library, their faces etched with worry and impatience. Officer Runt paced back and forth, his radio crackling. The parents exchanged anxious glances, their eyes darting to the library's entrance every few seconds, hoping for any sign of their children.

Mrs. Eldrod clutched her husband's arm, her knuckles white. "They've been in there too long," she whispered, her voice trembling. Mr. Eldrod nodded; his jaw clenched in silent agreement.

Nearby, Mrs. Hayes wiped away tears with a trembling hand, her gaze fixed on the library's shadowy interior. "Why did they go in there?" she murmured, more to herself than anyone else. Mr. Hayes placed a comforting hand on her shoulder, though his own eyes betrayed his fear.

The air was thick with tension, the only sounds the distant hum of the city and the occasional rustle of leaves in the wind. The parents' hearts pounded in unison, each second feeling like an eternity as they waited for their children to emerge from the darkness.

Suddenly, a faint noise echoed from within the library. The parents and officers froze, straining to hear. The sound grew louder, a series of muffled thumps and then, they heard a window shatter. The parents rushed towards it, their relief palpable as they saw their children, dusty and shaken, and bloody. The parents exchanged uneasy glances, their relief mingling with a new sense of unease. As they led their children away from the library, Officer Runt stayed behind, his gaze fixed on the darkened entrance. He couldn't shake the feeling that the mystery of the abandoned library was far from over.

Amber's mother, stood at there, her face a mask of worry and desperation. She rushed towards them, her voice trembling. "Where is Amber? Where is my daughter?"

Hope, her face pale and streaked with tears, stepped forward. "Mrs. Wilde, we... we tried to save her. The spirits..."

Asher, his hands shaking, added, "We were all together, but then... something didn't let us help her. We couldn't reach her in time."

Josh and Evan exchanged a haunted look, their silence speaking volumes. Amber's mom's eyes darted between them, her fear mounting. "What do you mean? Where is she?"

Evan finally spoke, his voice barely above a whisper. "She's gone, Mrs. Eldrod. The ghost... it took her."

A gasp escaped Mrs. Eldrod's lips as she clutched her chest, her knees buckling. "No... no, this can't be true."

Hope reached out, her own tears falling freely. "We're so sorry. We tried everything, but the library... it's cursed."

The group stood in a somber silence, the weight of their loss pressing down on them. The night seemed to grow colder, the shadows deeper, as the reality of Amber's fate settled over them like a dark shroud. "What happened in there?" Mrs. Eldrod whispered, brushing Hope's hair away from her eyes.

"Are these the children, ma'am?" Officer Runt came.

"Yes, sir." Mrs. Eldrod trembled.

"Alright. Come with us. We'll need to interrogate you guys. Wait--where's the last one? You've reported 5 missing children. There are only four here."

Everyone went silent. Nobody knew how to explain the death of Amber.

"She's gone, sir." Amber's mom spoke.

"I'm sorry?"

"Fedora killed her." Josh said.

"Fedora? Was she another child in there?" Officer Runt furrowed his eyebrows.

"No, sir. We'll explain everything, but first, can we please sit down?" Hope panted.

"Of course." He led them to the front of the library, to sit at the stairs where they all were previously sitting. "Here," He handed them each a bottle of water. "Thank you." They said in unison. They drank the whole bottle of water and then, Hope put the bottles in her bag. "Alright, now. Tell us everything that happened in there."

"Well," Hope began.

***

"So, you're telling me that a girl named Fedora Blinkan died in there and she was making you guys do all sorts of ridiculous tasks, in order to get revenge on her murderer and when Amber got possessed, she didn't tell you where to find the bananas in order to save her so, she died?" Officer Runt summarized, after Hope told the tale.

"Yes, sir."

"My main question is, Josh, Evan, what was the need for Hope to prove herself in the first place? Why did you need to go into the library in the first place? We've closed it off for a reason." Officer Runt asked.

"Sir, Hope isn't popular and we thought that Asher should be friends with someone more popular so that we wouldn't get bullied. We thought the library would be the perfect way to make sure Asher realized how much of a scaredy cat Hope was. But obviously, that backfired." Evan explained.

"But that doesn't change the fact that library is still permanently closed. But, after hearing your story, we're obviously not going to arrest you guys. But we will have an investigation in the library."

"NO!" The kids shouted in unison. "You can't risk your life like that, Officer! You don't know what's in there!"

That was when the parents realized how traumatized everyone became. "Hope, Asher, Josh, Evan. It's okay. You're out of there now. You're alright!" Mrs. Eldrod tried to calm everyone down.

"But Amber's not." Amber's mom whispered. "You all were blaming my daughter for this, right? Well, look what's happened. I'm not blaming your children for my daughter's death, but I'd like it if you guys would acknowledge the fact that my daughter was supposedly at fault here, but now, she's dead!" She stood up.

"Kelly, we're extremely sorry. We can understand your pain--"

"No, you can't! Your kids are alive!" She sobbed. Hope, Asher, Josh and Evan got up and hugged Amber's mom.

"Mrs. Wilde, we're really sorry. If Fedora had just told us where those bananas were, we could've saved her." Hope said.

Amber's mom didn't say anything. She hugged Hope tightly. So tightly that Hope couldn't breathe. "Hope, I'm not blaming you. Any of you. I'm just angry. My daughter didn't deserve this."

"We know."

"We'll have to go and get her body out of there." Officer Runt said.

"Don't bother. She's probably already a ghost by now." Josh said.

"Yeah. Fedora just collects bodies." Asher added.

"Really?" Amber's mom asked, tears still in her eyes.

"Yeah." Hope agreed.

"Well, I'm happy you're all alive." She hugged them all again, their parents smiling as they watched.

CHAPTER XIV

Goodbye, Amber

'I felt guilty as hell. No one could've prepared me for this. When I said I wanted to kill her, I didn't mean literally! I had read a quote once: "Don't stop the problem. Find the root cause and end it." I've tried to end the problem, but now, I've ended the root cause. Someone could argue that it was my fault and I wouldn't back down because it is my fault. I should've listened to Asher and not have gone in there. Mrs. Wilde forgave us, but I haven't forgiven myself. I especially feel bad for Josh. He and Amber were like me and Asher. Officer Runt has started an investigation, despite us telling him not to. I'm worried for him and his team but for now, I'm standing here, watching them bury Amber's body. Officer Runt had gone in and retrieved her body so that Amber would have a proper funeral. I'm here, crying next to Mom, Dad and Asher. I can't believe that this day has actually come, though. I never thought I'd witness Amber's death, let alone her funeral. I'm sorry, Amber. I really don't think you deserved this. I never thought you should've died like this. If anyone had to die, it should have been Fedora--but wait...never mind. You get my point, right, Amber?' Hope thought.

As the priest spoke solemn words of farewell, Hope's mind drifted back to the countless times Amber had tormented her. The cruel words, the mocking laughter, the isolation. Yet, standing here now, all those memories seemed insignificant compared to the overwhelming sadness she felt for Amber's untimely death.

Hope's eyes welled up with tears as she thought about the pain Amber must have been hiding behind her tough exterior. She wondered if things could have been different if she had reached out, if she had tried to understand Amber instead of just enduring her cruelty. The regret gnawed at her, a constant reminder of missed opportunities for compassion.

She took a deep breath and stepped forward, placing a single white rose on the casket. "I'm sorry, Amber," she whispered, her voice trembling. "I'm sorry for everything."

As the final prayers were said and the crowd began to disperse, Hope lingered a moment longer, her heart aching for the girl who had caused her so much pain. In that moment, she realized that forgiveness wasn't just about letting go of the past, but also about finding peace within herself.

'I feel so bad! I didn't think Amber would die like this. Standing next to Hope, I couldn't shake the feeling of guilt gnawing at me. Here I was, at the funeral of Amber, the girl who made Hoppy's life a living hell, and all I could think about was how brutally she was killed. The memories of her taunts and cruel jokes flooded my mind, and I couldn't help but think of how she didn't deserve this. I glanced around, seeing the somber faces of her family and friends. They were mourning a loss, but all I could remember was the pain she caused. My thoughts were a tangled mess. Part of me wanted to leave, to escape the awkwardness and the weight of my own conscience. But another part of me knew that staying was the right thing to do, even if it felt ridiculously bad. Maybe, just maybe, this was a step towards forgiveness, not just for him, but for myself too.' Asher thought.

Everyone watched as Amber's coffin was being buried in the ground, her grave reading 'Amber Wilde, beloved friend and daughter. 2006-2022'

Epilogue

The library was completely lifeless except for the ghosts haunting it. The library was laid out in a labyrinthine fashion, with rows upon rows of towering bookshelves creating narrow, winding aisles. Each shelf was packed with books of all sizes and ages, their spines showing the wear of countless hands that had once sought their knowledge. In the center of the main hall, there was a large reading area with heavy wooden tables and plush, albeit dusty, armchairs. Chandeliers hung from the ceiling, their crystals dulled by time, casting ghostly shadows in the dim light.

Hidden alcoves and private reading nooks were scattered throughout, offering secluded spots for quiet study. The mezzanine level housed rare and ancient manuscripts, accessible by a series of narrow, creaky staircases. The air was thick with the scent of old paper and leather, mingling with the faint, lingering aroma of ink.

Despite its state of abandonment, the library's architecture and layout spoke of a time when it had been a bustling hub of intellectual activity, a place where stories and knowledge were cherished and shared.

The air was thick with the musty scent of aged paper and forgotten stories.

In the heart of this forsaken place lay a thick, ancient book. Its leather cover was worn and cracked, yet it exuded an aura of mystery and power. This book held Amber's story and soul; her essence intertwined with its pages. The book seemed to pulse with a faint, otherworldly glow, as if it breathed with a life of its own.

The library, once a beacon of light and learning, now felt haunted. Shadows danced along the walls, and the faintest echoes of Amber's voice could be heard, telling her tale to anyone who dared to listen. The atmosphere was both melancholic and enchanting, a testament to the life that once was and the stories that remained. The officers entered, ready to investigate when they saw the book first. They opened it and read about all the poor souls who had come here to die. They were reading when they heard something. "Hello!" A girl said, "I'm Amber. I died when I was 16. Who are you?"

Acknowlededgments

'The cursed library' was an idea that I had gotten earlier in the year. I started to plan the whole thing in a document and then, once done, I started to write.

First and foremost, I would like to thank my parents and my sister for helping me throughout the journey of writing. Your belief in me kept me going even when I doubted myself.

I am also indebted to Thea, my dear friend, whose support and ideas were invaluable in shaping this book. Your expertise and dedication have made this work far better than I could have achieved alone.

Finally, I want to thank my friends, Anvika and Meghna for showing so much enthusiasm when I told them I was writing this book. Your enthusiasm and interest have been a driving force behind this book.

Thank you all for being a part of this journey. This book would not have been possible without your support.